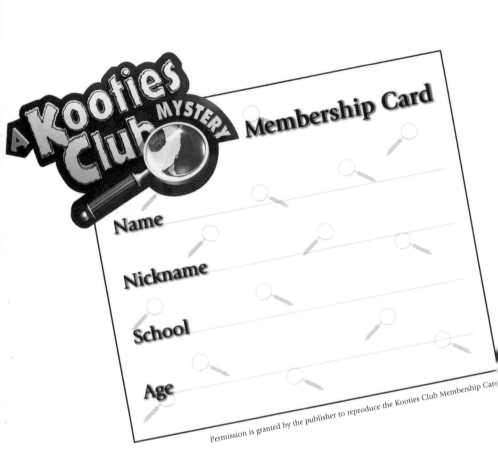

A Kooties Club MYSTERY

Membership Card

Name

Nickname

School

Age

The Mystery of the Gross Gift

by M. J. Cosson

Perfection Learning® CA

Cover and Inside Illustrations: Michael A. Aspengren

For information, contact
Perfection Learning® Corporation,
1000 North Second Avenue, P.O. Box 500,
Logan, Iowa 51546-0500.
Phone: 1-800-831-4190 • Fax: 1-712-644-2392
Paperback 0-7891-2875-6
Cover Craft® 0-7807-7838-3
7 8 9 10 11 12 PP 11 10 09 08 07 06

Table of Contents

Introduction

Abe, Ben, Gabe, Toby, and Ty live in a large city. There isn't much for kids to do. There isn't even a park close by.

Their neighborhood is made up of apartment houses and trailer parks. Gas stations and small shops stand where the parks and grass used to be. And there aren't many houses with big yards.

Ty and Abe live in an apartment complex. Next door is a large vacant lot. It is full of brush, weeds, and trash. A path runs across the lot. On the other side is a trailer park. Ben and Toby live there.

Across the street from the trailer park is a big gray house. Gabe lives in the top apartment of the house.

The five boys have known each other since they started school. But they haven't always been friends.

The other kids say the boys have cooties. And the other kids won't touch them with a ten-foot pole. So Abe, Ben, Gabe, Toby, and Ty have formed their own club. They call it the Kooties Club.

Here's how to join. If no one else will have anything to do with you, you're in.

The boys call themselves the Koots for short. Ben's grandma calls his grandpa an *old coot*. And Ben thinks his grandpa is pretty cool. So if he's an old coot, Ben and his friends must be young koots.

The Koots play ball and hang out with each other. But most of all, they look for mysteries to solve.

Chapter 1

The Gift

Mr. Dodge held out the box. Abe looked away. But Ty looked closer.

"Looks like a heart," Ty said. "I saw pictures of one in a science book."

Mr. Dodge touched the object in the box. He had on a pair of thin plastic gloves. They were the kind doctors wear.

"Dog is a good hunter," Mr. Dodge said. His big cat, Dog, sat beside him.

Dog looked pleased with himself. He had given his friend a good gift. Dog licked his fur.

"I thought it might be a heart," Mr. Dodge said. "But it also feels like an animal with no fur or feathers."

Mr. Dodge touched the heart again. He was blind. Touch was one way he learned things.

"No. It's a heart for sure," said Ty, looking even closer.

Abe said, "Gross." He felt sick. So he sat down.

"Hmmm," said Mr. Dodge. "I wonder where Dog got this. And what kind of animal it belongs to. I think it's too small to belong to a person."

"It could be a kid's heart," said Ty. Abe shuddered.

11

"I doubt it," said Mr. Dodge. "I've had cats bring in mice or birds," he went on. "But they always bring the whole animal."

"Hmmm," said Abe. He put the picture of a bird in his mind instead of a kid. That helped him feel better.

"Is there a butcher shop around here?" asked Mr. Dodge.

Both Ty and Abe shook their heads. "Nope. No butcher shop. No grocery store either," said Ty.

"It's a mystery," said Mr. Dodge. Ty and Abe looked at each other and grinned. Maybe the Kooties Club could solve it.

"We'll find out where it came from, Mr. Dodge," promised Ty.

When Abe opened the door to leave, Dog ran out. He ran down the apartment stairs fast. In a flash, he was gone.

Half an hour later, all the Koots were in Ty's apartment. Ty was telling the others about the heart. The telephone rang.

"Hello," said Ty.

He listened for a minute. "We'll be right there," he said. He hung up the phone.

"Mr. Dodge just got another gift from Dog," he told the Koots.

"Let's go!" said Gabe.

13

Chapter 2

Another Gift

A few minutes later, the Koots stood around Mr. Dodge. Once again, he held out a box. This time there was something different in it. The kids didn't know what it was.

Dog sat beside Mr. Dodge. He looked very pleased with himself.

"Where is Dog getting all of this?" asked Toby.

"That's what I want to know," replied Mr. Dodge.

"When we left," said Abe, "Dog went out too. He was in a hurry. He must have run straight to where he finds the stuff."

"Let's follow him," suggested Gabe. He looked ready to start running.

Abe opened the door. Gabe ran out. Ty was right behind him. Then Ben ran out after Ty. Toby ran behind Ben. Abe stood holding the door.

Dog still sat next to Mr. Dodge. He licked his fur. Mr. Dodge could hear that Dog was still there.

"He must be done hunting for today," said Mr. Dodge.

The Koots all stood in the doorway.

"Come on, Dog!" they yelled. "Let's go! Let's go find more guts."

But Dog just looked at them.

Finally Toby said, "We'll go look around. Maybe tomorrow Dog will want to hunt again."

Mr. Dodge laughed. "Isn't that just like a cat? They sure have minds of their own. They never do what you want them to. I'll see you guys tomorrow."

"No, Mr. Dodge. We'll see you," said the Koots as they left. It was an

old joke between the Koots and their blind friend.

Abe shut the door. The Koots walked down the stairs. They were thinking. Just where was Dog hunting? And to whom or what did the unusual parts belong?

"I know!" said Ben. "Maybe Mrs. Purdy's dog can help us."

The Koots walked to Mrs. Purdy's trailer. They knocked, and she opened her door. Ben explained the mystery.

"Has Elvis brought home any guts lately?" asked Ben. Elvis was Mrs. Purdy's dog.

"No, boys. Sorry. I don't let Elvis wander." Mrs. Purdy shook her head. "And what do you mean by guts?" she asked.

"You know. Insides," said Gabe.

"Like livers and hearts and blood and . . ." added Toby.

"Guts," Abe finished for him.

"My, no," said Mrs. Purdy. She put her hands on her cheeks. She shook her head.

"Mr. Lopez's dog wanders," she said. "You could ask him."

"Thanks, Mrs. Purdy," said the Koots. They headed over to Lopezes' trailer.

Gabe knocked, and the door opened a crack. Mr. Lopez peered out.

"Hi, Mr. Lopez," said Toby. "Has your dog brought any gifts home lately?"

Mr. Lopez looked surprised. "What?" he asked.

18

"Has your dog brought home any guts?" said Gabe.

"No!" Mr. Lopez shouted. He slammed the door.

The Koots walked away from the trailer. They kept looking back at the closed door.

"He's spooky," said Ty. "He acted pretty funny."

"He always acts that way," said Ben. "Most kids are afraid of him."

"I'll bet he knows something," said Toby.

"Maybe he killed something," added Gabe.

"Or someone," said Abe.

Chapter 3

Fright in the Night

The Koots walked to Toby's trailer. They sat on the steps. It was almost time for supper.

"Now what?" asked Ben.

"We could spy on Mr. Lopez," said Ty.

"What if he's a killer?" asked Abe.

"We could be in big trouble if he catches us," said Toby.

"We need a bloodhound," said Gabe.

"What's a bloodhound?" asked Abe. He began to feel sick again. "Does it bleed?"

"Everything bleeds, you goof," said Ty, chuckling. He stopped and thought. "Well, most animals bleed," he added.

"Bloodhounds track down things," explained Ben. "They help the police find bad guys. They sniff out drugs too."

"Yeah," said Toby. "A bloodhound could help us find the guts. It would sniff them out."

Gabe stood up. "How about Ruth?" he asked.

"Who's Ruth?" asked Ty.

"You know, that dog on my street," Gabe said. "The brown dog with the long ears and short legs. She's a basset hound. That's kind of like a bloodhound.

"She sniffs real good," Gabe added. "Her owners let me take her for walks. Tomorrow morning, I'll ask to walk her. We can meet here at nine."

Just then Toby's mom came to the door. "Time for supper, Toby. Tonight is your night to wash dishes. Then you have to do your homework. No waiting until Sunday night." She smiled.

Toby looked at the other Koots. He made a face. "See you guys tomorrow morning," he said.

22

The sun had gone down. And the sky was almost black. There were a few stars in the sky.

Ty and Abe cut across the deserted lot. They didn't talk. Ty was thinking about the guts. Where did they come from? Did they belong to a person?

Abe was wondering if Mr. Lopez had a big knife. Mr. Lopez might jump out at them. He would use the knife on them. Maybe next time Dog would bring **his** guts home to Mr. Dodge. Abe screamed. He began to run. Ty ran too.

Gabe walked through the other side of the lot toward his house. He had to walk alone. He walked along the path. A loud scream broke the quiet. Was someone being killed?

Gabe started to run. All of a sudden, he slipped and fell. His hand touched something slick and gooey. Had he slipped in a pool of bloody guts?

Gabe jumped up. He ran as fast as he could. He knew the killer was right behind him!

At last Gabe got home. He slammed the door shut. He was shaking. He looked at his pants. They were dark and wet. And there was blood on his hand!

Chapter 4

Ruth the Sleuth

Saturday morning Gabe got up and got dressed. His hand still hurt. He must have cut it on something when he fell.

Gabe's mom had been mad. His pants were covered with mud. And he had tracked mud all through the house.

Gabe had had a hard time explaining to his mom what had happened. He still wasn't sure if she believed him or not.

"Oh, well. At least I'm safe from the killer," he thought.

Gabe ate a quick breakfast. Then he ran down the street to Ruth's house. He felt much safer in the daylight.

"We'll be back in about an hour," Gabe promised the dog's owner. He walked down the street with Ruth. This time Gabe took the sidewalk. Not the vacant lot.

The Koots were waiting in front of the trailer court.

"Hey," said Toby. "This is a great bloodhound!"

"Lead us to the guts, Ruth," said Gabe. He started walking to the deserted lot. Ruth followed.

The Koots walked all over the vacant lot. They dragged Ruth behind them. She was an old dog. She was tired. She didn't seem to care about finding guts.

At last, Toby said, "Gabe, this dog is no good. She's lazy. We can work faster without her."

Everyone agreed.

"Come with me to take her home," said Gabe. "Then we can go see Mr. Dodge. Maybe Dog is ready for another hunting trip."

The Koots walked Ruth down the street. They saw a big dog coming toward them. The dog passed them. They could see that he had something in his mouth.

The dog growled, and it began to run.

"It looked like a huge bone to me," said Toby. "He must have found the bone over there." Toby pointed down the block.

The Koots returned Ruth. Then they walked down the street. They came to an old, deserted house. The yard was full of weeds. The Koots looked for clues in the yard. They spent all morning hunting. But they didn't find any guts.

Ty pointed to an open window. A board had once covered it. But now the board was lying on the ground.

"Do you think there's a body in there?" he asked.

Chapter 5

The Deserted House

"Call me turkey," said Abe. "But I'm not going in there."

"You mean chicken," said Ben. "Me neither. I think we should call the police."

"Why should we call the police?" asked Gabe. "We don't know for sure whether there's a body in the house."

"The house should be boarded up," said Ben.

"I'm going in," said Ty. "Anybody with me?"

"I'll go," said Gabe.

"I'll stand watch," said Toby.

Ben turned to walk away. "I'm going to call the police. You guys could get hurt in there," he said.

"I'm coming with you, Ben," said Abe.

Ben and Abe walked down the street.

Ty went to the window. "Give me a boost," he said.

Toby bent over. Ty stood on his back. He reached up to the window. He pulled himself up and looked in.

31

The house was dark. Ty dragged himself through the window. Gabe followed.

The two boys stood in the dark room. Slowly, their eyes got used to the dark.

They spied a doorway across the room. They crept toward it. When they got to the doorway, they peeked around.

There was a long, dark hall. They walked slowly down it.

When they got to the other end, they stopped in front of a door. There was no sound. But both Ty and Gabe had the strange feeling that they were not alone.

They stood still for a few minutes. Carefully, Ty pushed the door open.

32

Ty peeked around the edge of the door. The windows were all boarded up. The room was as dark as the hallway.

Was something in the corner? Yes. It looked like a person. It was sitting on the floor. Its back was against the wall. But it didn't move.

Ty was afraid to go closer. Gabe stuck his head in the doorway. He saw it too. Both boys stood still.

"Hello, boys," the body said.

Ty and Gabe screamed. They slammed the door shut and ran back up the hall. They turned and ran through the other room and dove out the window. Ty fell on Toby. Gabe fell on top of both of them.

33

Ty and Gabe jumped up. They ran down the street. Toby limped after them. His leg was sore from Ty falling on him.

The boys met Ben and Abe coming up the street. They stopped running. They looked behind them. No one was chasing them.

"What's wrong?" asked Ben. "You look like you've seen a ghost."

"Maybe," said Gabe, trying to catch his breath. His eyes were big. He and Ty told the other three what had happened.

"Well, the police are on their way," said Ben. "They'll see what's in that spooky old house."

Chapter 6

The Search

At last, the police came. The Koots met them in front of the deserted house.

"Are you the kids who called?" asked the tall police officer.

"Yes," said Abe. "He called." He pointed to Ben.

"What's going on?" asked the shorter officer.

"Someone is in that house," said Gabe.

The tall police officer looked in the window.

"Anybody in there?" he yelled. There was no answer.

"Well, I guess we'd better go in and check it out," he said loudly.

Not a sound came from inside the house. The officer pulled himself through the window. His partner stayed outside with the Koots.

A few minutes later, the officer crawled back out the window. "There's no one in there," he said. "We better get this board back on," he added.

His partner looked at the Koots. "You kids go find somewhere else to play. This old house is unsafe."

37

"But somebody is in there," insisted Gabe.

"Maybe I was wrong," said the tall officer loudly. "Maybe someone is in there. If so, they'll be gone soon," he said. "Now you kids get out of here."

The Koots walked away from the old house.

"I know someone is in there," said Gabe.

"So why didn't the police find him? Or her? Or it?" asked Toby.

No one had an answer.

"We should tell them about the guts and everything," said Ben.

"They won't believe us," said Gabe. "We're just kids."

"Let's go see Mr. Dodge. Maybe he'll talk to them. They'd believe him," said Ben.

38

Finally the Koots got to Mr. Dodge's apartment. They told him about the old house. And what they had heard.

Mr. Dodge shook his head. "It is a mystery," he said.

"Has Dog brought home any more surprises?" asked Ty.

"No," said Mr. Dodge. "I've kept him in all morning so you could follow him. And he's been wanting to go out."

"Okay, then," said Gabe. He stood by the door, ready to run a race.

"Open the door!" he shouted.

Toby opened the door. Dog shot out. Gabe ran after him. Ben, Ty, Toby, and Abe followed. Mr. Dodge wheeled himself over to the door.

"Be careful!" he yelled after the boys.

Chapter 7

Follow That Cat!

Dog ran down the steps and across the parking lot. He ran through the deserted lot. He ran down the street the Koots had just been on. The Koots followed.

Dog ran between two houses. Then he slipped under a tall wood fence. The Koots were blocked. The fence was too high.

"We'll run around this way. You guys go that way," Gabe yelled.

Each boy took off. Abe lay on the ground. He tried to look under the fence. But he couldn't see anything. It was too late. Dog was gone.

The boys walked around. They yelled, "Here, Dog!" But they all knew it was useless. Most cats don't come when they're called.

For the next hour, the Koots searched for Dog. They walked through all the yards. But they stayed away from the deserted house. They could see that the board was still off the window.

At last, they started back toward the apartments. When they got to the deserted lot, Ty turned around. Dog was behind them. He was dragging something long. The Koots ran toward him.

41

"Yuck," they all cried.

Dog was dragging a long string of something gross. It was gray. And it seemed to glow in the sunshine.

"Ick!" said Abe.

"Intestines!" said Gabe.

"Guts!" said Ty.

"Now what are we going to do?" asked Ben.

"Let's take them away from him," said Toby. "Maybe he'll go get more."

"There's an old coffee can," said Gabe, pointing toward the vacant lot. "Maybe we can scoop them into the can with a stick."

"Great idea!" said Ty. He moved toward the cat. Dog stopped moving forward. He began stepping backward.

Toby bent down to pick up Dog. Dog growled just like a dog.

42

"Maybe that's how he got his name," said Toby. "I'm not going to pick him up. He might bite like a dog too."

"Okay," said Ty. "We'll wait. Sooner or later, he'll drop them."

The boys surrounded Dog. Dog looked from one boy to the next. But he hung on to the intestines.

Dog sat down. The Koots waited. After a while, the big cat lay down. He still had the string of guts in his mouth. The Koots waited.

Finally, Dog took a cat nap. His big eyes closed.

Ty whispered, "I'm going to pull them away with the stick."

He bent over. He hooked the intestines with the stick. He pulled.

The guts popped out of Dog's mouth.
But Dog woke up.

Ty flipped the guts into the coffee
can. Dog jumped. He clawed Ty. He
went "Ftttt!"

Ty ran down the street. Dog
chased after him. The rest of the
Koots followed.

Ty threw the can over a fence. He
stopped, and Dog stopped next to
him.

Dog didn't know where the can
had gone. He looked at Ty. And Ty
stared back.

Finally, Dog turned around. He
walked slowly down the street. The
Koots followed him.

45

Chapter 8

Dog Leads the Way

Dog went to the deserted house. But he didn't go inside. He went one house farther. He walked to a tipped-over trash can.

The Koots looked inside. Bones and guts spilled from the can.

The Koots watched Dog grab more intestines. He began to drag them home.

"Okay, now it's time to call the police," said Toby.

Everyone agreed.

Gabe's house was closest. So he ran home to make the call. Abe went with him. He was tired of feeling sick. He didn't want to be near the guts.

The other Koots stood guard. They watched Dog walk off with his new treat.

Ben yelled after Gabe, "Call Mr. Dodge. Tell him Dog is on his way home with another gift!"

From where they stood, the Koots could see the deserted house. They could see the open window. Toby stared at the window. All of a sudden, he jumped.

"I saw something in that window!" he said. "Something moved. I'm sure."

Ben and Ty watched the house. They saw it too. Something was inside that house!

Chapter 9

The Trash

At last, Gabe and Abe came back.

"Here comes the police car," said Abe. He ran out to the street. In a few minutes, he came back. The same two officers were with him.

"What now, kids?" asked one of the officers.

"We found these guts," said Toby. He pointed to the trash.

The officers looked closely at the guts.

"So you think someone has been killed?" one of the officers asked.

"We think so," said Abe. "That's somebody's insides."

Toby pointed to the deserted house. "And we think the person who did it is in that house," he said.

"Or maybe it's Mr. Lopez," added Abe.

"I told you kids, that house is empty," said the tall officer.

"We know someone is in there," said Ben. "We just saw someone in that window."

"Let's get this settled," said the short officer. He walked to the back door of the closest house. When he knocked, a man came to the door.

The two talked. Then the officer and the man walked toward the Koots.

"Yes, sir. This is my trash," answered the man.

"And whose intestines are those?" asked the officer.

The man looked at the guts. He looked at the officer. He looked at the Koots. Then he set the trash can back up. He put on the lid.

"Do you know whose intestines those are?" asked the short officer again.

"Yes, sir," said the man. "I hit a deer with my car. I killed it. I felt bad. But I didn't want the meat to go to waste. It is in my freezer. This is what was left."

"Did you report the accident?" asked the other officer.

52

"No," said the man.

"You'll need to fill out a report," said the officer. "We'll have to call the conservation office to see if you've broken the law."

"Okay, kids," said the short police officer. "The mystery is solved. You can go home now."

"So these are deer guts?" asked Ty.

"Yes," answered the officer. He and his partner walked toward their car.

"What about the killer?" Gabe yelled after them. The officers just turned and waved.

"I'm the killer of the deer," said the man.

"But what about the killer who's living in the deserted house?" asked Ben. He pointed to the old house.

53

"That's just Old Jim," said the man. "He wouldn't hurt a fly."

"So you know someone is in that house?" asked Toby.

"Sure," said the man.

"Do the police know he's there?" asked Ty.

"I think so. Every once in a while, someone from the city puts the board back on the house. But Old Jim just takes it off again," said the man.

"Old Jim has nowhere else to live," he added.

Toby turned to the rest of the Koots. "I guess this case is closed," he said.

"Not yet," said Gabe. "We have to tell Mr. Dodge."

Chapter 10

The Story

The intestines sat in a box on Mr. Dodge's floor. Dog sat beside them. With a lot of hard work, the cat had pulled the present up the stairs and into his home. He looked very proud and very tired.

The Koots were sitting on the floor in front of Mr. Dodge. They were telling what happened.

"So then, the police put yellow tape around the crime scene," said Gabe.

"And they took the guy away to jail," said Toby.

"Dog will be a hero for helping us solve the crime," said Ty.

"And we'll all be on the six o'clock news," said Ben.

"Do you want me to turn on the TV?" asked Abe.

"No," said Mr. Dodge. He smiled. "Now tell me what really happened."

The Koots all laughed.